KEISHA DISCOVERS HARLEM
by Zoe Lewis

Illustrations by
Dan Burr

Spot Illustrations by
Rich Grote

MAGIC ATTIC PRESS

Published by Magic Attic Press.

For more information contact:
Book Editor, Magic Attic Press, 866 Spring Street,
Westbrook, ME 04092-3808

First Edition
Printed in the United States of America
1 2 3 4 5 6 7 8 9 10

Magic Attic Club® is a registered trademark.

Betsy Gould, Publisher
Marva Martin, Art Director
Jay Brady, Managing Editor

Edited by Judit Bodnar
Designed by Cindy Vacek

Lewis, Zoe
Keisha Discovers Harlem / by Zoe Lewis:
illustrations by Dan Burr, spot illustrations by Rich Grote
(Magic Attic Club)
Summary: When Keisha put on the shimmering flapper dress, she had no idea her
adventure would land her in Harlem in the 1920's. Keisha is asked to be an apprentice
reporter and cover the Young Musician's Contest. Will Keisha get the story?
ISBN 1-57513-130-7 (hardback) ISBN 1-57513-129-3 (paperback)
ISBN 1-57513-144-7 (library edition hardback)

Library of Congress Cataloging in Publication Data is on file at the Library of Congress

As members of the
MAGIC ATTIC CLUB,
we promise to
be best friends,
share all of our adventures in the attic,
use our imaginations,
have lots of fun together,
and remember—the real magic is in us.

Alison *Keisha*

Heather *Megan*

Rose

Table of Contents

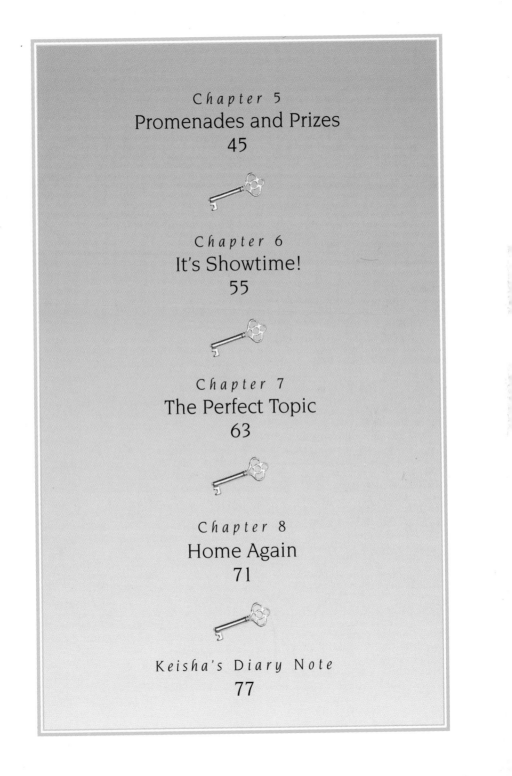

Prologue

When Alison, Heather, Keisha, and Megan find a
golden key buried in the snow, they have no idea that
it will change their lives forever. They discover that it
belongs to Ellie Goodwin, the owner of an old
Victorian house across the street from Alison's. Ellie,
grateful when they return the key to her, invites the
girls to play in her attic. There they find a steamer
trunk filled with wonderful outfits—party dresses, a
princess gown, a ballet tutu, cowgirl clothes, and
many, many, more. The girls try on some of the
costumes and admire their reflections in a tall, gilded
mirror nearby. Suddenly they are transported to a new
time and place, embarking on the greatest adventure
of their lives.

After they return to the present and Ellie's attic,
they form the Magic Attic Club, promising to tell
each other every exciting detail of their future
adventures. Then they meet Rose Hopkins, a new
girl at school, and invite her to join the club and
share their amazing secret.

Chapter

One

AN INTERESTING
ASSIGNMENT

hat time period are you going to pick, Keisha?"
Heather Hardin asked.

Keisha Vance shrugged and swung her bookbag back
and forth. "I'm not sure," she admitted. "I guess I'll have
to think about it."

"It's a really neat assignment." Megan Ryder's green
eyes were sparkling with excitement. She hopped over a
large crack in the sidewalk. "I'm glad Ms. Austin thought
of it. My only problem is going to be choosing just *one*

period in American history to write about. There are so many important times and places when it would have been interesting to live."

Alison McCann and Rose Hopkins nodded. Keisha nodded, too, but she sighed at the same time. The truth was, she had no idea what topic to choose—not because she had too many ideas, like Megan, but because she didn't have *any*. She had been thinking about it ever since her fifth-grade teacher had announced the assignment. She and her friends had been talking about it ever since they had all left Lincoln Elementary School for their afternoon walk home.

"I didn't have any trouble deciding what to write about," Alison declared, shoving her blond bangs out of her eyes and grinning at her four best friends. "The American Revolution. Definitely." She waved her arms excitedly as she talked, almost bonking Rose on the head. "Minutemen, Paul Revere, Valley Forge—all that stuff always sounds so exciting."

Heather laughed. "That doesn't surprise me, Ali," she teased. "It figures you would want to be where the action is."

Keisha laughed, too. Alison was

a very adventurous person, so it made perfect sense that she would pick one of the most adventurous times in history to write about.

"What are you doing for your project, Heather?" Rose asked.

"That's easy," Heather said. "My grandparents—my mom's mom and dad, I mean—used to tell me about coming to the United States from Poland in the 1930s. They came through Ellis Island with immigrants from all over the world. I'm going to write about that."

"That sounds really interesting," Rose agreed. "I think I'm going to write about the Cheyenne in the mid-1800s. I'm sure my grandfather can help me with the research."

Keisha nodded. "That's great, Rose," she said wistfully as the five friends turned the corner onto Primrose Lane. "You and Heather are both picking topics that have to do with your family roots. That makes the project even better."

"You could do that, too," Megan suggested. "Did any of your relatives travel on the Underground Railroad or fight in the Civil War or anything like that?"

Keisha shrugged. "A few." She had always tried to learn everything she could about the members of her family from long-ago generations. She knew that a number of them had been involved in the fight to end slavery in the United States. "But I don't think I want to write about that stuff," she went on. "It was definitely a very interesting time in history. But for some reason it just seems kind of—well—obvious."

"What do you mean?" Alison looked surprised.

Keisha bit her lip and glanced at her friends as they all drifted to a stop in front of Heather's house. "You know, because I'm African-American. People always think the Civil War and the emancipation of the slaves is the only important history we have."

Megan looked hurt. "That's not what I meant," she said quickly. "It was just an idea. Maybe you could do the civil rights movement in the 1960s instead." Her smile returned. "Actually, I was thinking about picking the sixties myself. There was an awful lot of stuff happening then—you know, the Vietnam War, hippies, rock and roll... although I might decide to write about the women's rights movement in the 1970s instead."

Keisha remained silent as the other four girls talked about Megan's ideas. She should have known they wouldn't understand what she meant—she wasn't sure she understood it herself. All she knew was that she wouldn't have wanted to live during a war, not even a war that was as

important to the people of the United States, black and white, as the Civil War. Maybe Alison would have enjoyed living then, since she loved action and excitement so much. Megan, too—she liked writing and journalism, so she could have reported on the war. Even Rose would have been fine. She never backed away from a fight if it was about something important.

But Keisha was a lot more interested in things like friends and music and reading and animals and photography than in fighting and war. That meant that if she wanted to be honest with Ms. Austin—and herself— she couldn't claim that she would have wanted to live during wartime, no matter how important the war was. And that was fine with her. Weren't there any peaceful times in America's past that were important? Why did people always think that the only interesting parts of history were wars?

She leaned against the streetlamp across from Heather's front walk and tugged absentmindedly on one of her long, black braids as she thought about Megan's other suggestion, the civil rights movement. The sixties did sound pretty interesting. But she didn't want to choose the same time period as Megan. She wanted a topic that would be all her own. One that would show her friends and classmates that there was more to African-American history than slavery and the Civil War. But what?

"I'd better go in now," Heather said a few minutes later, glancing over her shoulder at her house. "Mom's probably wondering what's taking me so long."

Suddenly Keisha realized that she had to hurry home, too. "Same here," she said. She didn't bother to explain why. Her friends knew that she baby-sat for her younger brother and sister after school when both of her parents were working.

"Okay," Alison said. "But listen, why don't we all meet at the library tomorrow to work on our assignments?"

Heather nodded eagerly. "Great idea, Ali," she agreed.

"I'll check with my parents and call you tonight."

"Me, too." Keisha grinned weakly. "I just hope I figure out a topic by then."

Megan reached over and gave Keisha's arm a friendly squeeze. "Don't worry," she said. "You know you can count on us to help you."

"That's right." Rose pushed her long, dark hair behind her shoulder and smiled at Keisha. "We can talk about it more at the library tomorrow."

Keisha nodded gratefully and said good-bye to her friends as they split up to head home. But as she hurried toward her own cozy brick house, she was still worried about the assignment. Maybe she should just write about the Civil War. Or maybe she *should* choose a time period that had nothing in particular to do with African-Americans at all.

"But what?" Keisha murmured to herself.

Chapter TWO

FAMILY HISTORY

eisha was setting the dinner table a couple of
hours later when she heard the front door open.
"Finish folding these napkins, okay, Ashley?" she urged
her five-year-old sister. "It sounds like Mom's home. That
means Daddy will be here soon."

But Ashley had already dropped her pile of cloth
napkins and was rushing toward the kitchen door. "I'll do
it in a minute," she cried. "I want to say hi!"

Two-year-old Ronnie looked up from the blocks he was

playing with in a corner of the big, bright kitchen. "Me, too! Me, too!" he shouted. He raced out of the room after Ashley as fast as his short, pudgy legs would carry him.

Keisha sighed. Sometimes it was hard being the oldest. She grabbed the napkins and hurriedly folded them herself. Then she went out to the front hall. Her mother, a nurse in the maternity ward of the local hospital, was patting  Ronnie's curly brown hair as he hugged her leg and giggled. Ashley was peering out the front window, watching for her father's car.

"Hi, Mom." Keisha grabbed the jacket her mother had draped over a ladderback chair and opened the hall closet.

"Hi, baby." Mrs. Vance smiled at Keisha, carefully loosened Ronnie's grip on her leg, and kicked off her white nurse's shoes. "Whew! What a day. I think every pregnant woman in town decided to have her baby during my shift today."

Keisha hung her mother's jacket carefully on a hanger, then closed the closet door and followed her down the hallway into the kitchen.

"Mama, I need to ask you about something," Keisha said as her mother bustled around the kitchen, continuing the dinner preparations that Keisha had started.

"Sure, Keisha-girl." Mrs. Vance opened the oven door and slid in a casserole dish. "What is it?"

Keisha sat down at the table and explained her assignment.

"That sounds interesting." Mrs. Vance smiled at Keisha before turning back to the stove. "Do you have any ideas yet?"

Keisha sighed. "No. I can't think of a single thing." She rested her elbows on the table. "History is so depressing!"

Mrs. Vance chuckled. "Well, some of it is, I'll give you that," she said. "But it's full of lots of good times, too, you know."

"Yeah, right." Keisha rolled her eyes. "Like what?"

Her mother stirred the pot of vegetables on the stove. "I have an idea," she said at last. "Why don't you and Daddy go through some of the old family photo albums tonight? Maybe seeing what our relatives did in the old days will give you some good ideas."

Keisha wrinkled her nose. "But I don't want to do the Underground Railroad or the Civil War," she said. "There's no way I would have wanted to live then. I hate wars."

"There's more to our family history than wars, honey," Mrs. Vance said gently as she continued to stir. "Just talk to your father, okay? I must confess, he knows a whole lot more about the family history than I do." She grinned at Keisha. "He can even keep track of my great-aunts and great-grandmas. I always get them all confused. I'm sure he can help you find something interesting to write about."

Keisha shrugged. She wasn't so sure about that. But what did she have to lose? "Okay," she said. "I'll talk to him."

"Can we go through the photo albums now?" Keisha asked her father after dinner.

Mr. Vance looked up from the kitchen sink. His arms were buried to the elbows in a mass of foamy, white soap bubbles. "Just another minute, Keisha-girl," he said. "I'm almost through with the pans."

"Mom?" Keisha turned to her mother, who was wiping crumbs off of Ronnie's round face. "You and I could start looking now."

"In a sec," Mrs. Vance replied. "I want to put the little ones to bed first. That way we won't be interrupted."

Keisha sighed impatiently. The minutes seemed to creep by as her father finished cleaning the kitchen and her mother coaxed Ashley and Ronnie upstairs and into their pajamas. But finally, the house was clean and quiet. Mr. and Mrs. Vance came downstairs to the living room after tucking in the younger children.

"Now?" Keisha demanded, jumping up from her seat on the couch.

Mr. Vance smiled and chucked her under the chin. "Sure, Keisha," he said. "We're all yours. Bring the albums over to the coffee table."

Keisha obeyed. She took a seat in the middle of the couch, and her parents sat down on either side of her.

"Here we go," Mr. Vance said cheerfully. "Time for an exciting trip back through the history of our family."

Keisha forced herself to smile. "Great," she said. Let's just hope the exciting family history includes something besides wars, she added to herself, leaning forward to look at the first page of photos.

"...and I think that's your great-grandpa Charles." Mrs. Vance paused and frowned, squinting at the blurry sepia-tone photograph on the page in front of her. "Or is it your great-great-uncle Bernard? I always get those two mixed up."

"It's Bernard," Mr. Vance said. "Definitely. See the cane? He had a bad leg."

Keisha examined the picture. The elderly man in it was scowling at the camera and clutching a walking stick. "What did he do?" she asked. "Did he live around here?"

Mrs. Vance shrugged helplessly and glanced at her husband again.

"He lived in Chicago most of his life," Mr. Vance said.

"He was in the navy, then he became a schoolteacher. He was quite a miser." He glanced at Keisha. "That means he hoarded his money and never spent a penny he didn't have to. Did I ever tell you about the time… "

Keisha smiled. Looking through the photos with her dad was fun, but they'd already spent almost two hours talking about her family's past and so far it seemed like a waste of time. Aside from the relatives she already knew about—like the ones who had traveled on the Underground Railroad during the time of slavery—nobody in her family seemed to have done anything that special.

And her father kept telling her stories that had nothing to do with her school project.

"Aha!" Mrs. Vance's eyes brightened when she spotted a large photo on the next page. "Now here's a snapshot I know something about."

Keisha took a closer look. "I've always meant to ask about this one," she said. "The ladies are wearing such cool dresses."

The black-and-white photograph, its edges rounded smooth by age, was of two women about Mrs. Vance's age. They were standing together on a crowded city street, their arms slung around each others' waists. But what drew Keisha's eye the most was their outfits. They wore short, fringed, boxy dresses, feathered hats, and shoes with low, chunky heels.

"The lady on the left is your great-grandma Ruth," Mrs. Vance explained. "This photo was taken during a trip she took to visit her dearest childhood friend, Norma Callister. Norma lived in Harlem—that's a section of New York City where a lot of African-Americans settled—and knew all the most interesting people there in the 1920s." She smiled. "She was quite a character, from the things I've heard."

"Like what?" Keisha asked, glancing again at Norma Callister's smiling face. "What did she do?"

"Norma was a great lady," Mr. Vance chimed in. His

eyes were wide with excitement, and Keisha could tell he was about to launch into another long story. "She knew everyone in Harlem during the Renaissance. That's the Harlem Renaissance," he explained. "It was a really important time in African-American history, especially for writers, artists, musicians, and—"

"Wait a minute, honey." Mrs. Vance smiled and held up a hand to stop her husband. "Your daddy could talk about the Harlem Renaissance for hours," she told Keisha. "But it's getting very late. We'd better stop here, and let him continue the history lesson tomorrow, after Ashley's tumbling meet."

Mr. Vance smiled sheepishly. "Your mother's right, honey. Norma Callister and the 1920s are two of my favorite topics, and I could go on all night. If the three of us want any sleep, I'd better stop right here."

Keisha nodded, feeling more disappointed than tired. She gave the photo one more glance, then flipped the album shut. Her mother seemed to sense her discouragement. "While we're out at Ashley's tumbling meet, why don't you look through Ellie Goodwin's books and see if you can get some more ideas?" she said to Keisha. "She's got quite an interesting library in that big old house of hers."

"That's true," Mr. Vance agreed with an approving nod. "She might even have some information on the Harlem Renaissance."

Keisha felt her spirits perk up. Why hadn't she thought of going to Ellie's herself? "That's a great idea!" she said.

Ellie Goodwin lived in a large Victorian house on Primrose Lane. When Keisha and her friends had gotten to know the older woman, they'd discovered that her rambling old house held a wonderful secret. Anytime one of the girls tried on one of the many interesting outfits in an old steamer trunk in her attic and then looked into the full-length mirror nearby, she was transported to another time and place. After their first adventure together in the attic, the friends had formed the Magic Attic Club. Since then, all five of them had enjoyed many exciting times in Ellie's amazing attic.

But the attic wasn't the only special thing about Ellie's house. Every room held treasures gathered during Ellie's lifetime of travel to fascinating, exotic places. There were photos, trinkets, posters, rugs—and books. Lots of books on every subject.

Keisha thanked her parents for their help, then hurried upstairs. Suddenly, she couldn't wait for the next day to arrive. First thing in the morning, she was going to call Ellie to ask if she could come over. Something told her that her idea was waiting in her friend's wonderful house.

"Hello, Mr. McCann. This is Keisha. Is Alison there?"
Keisha tapped her foot as she waited. She had just

spoken with Ellie, and although the conversation hadn't gone exactly as she'd planned, she was still trying to be optimistic.

"Hi, Keish," Alison greeted her over the phone. "What's up? You're still coming to the library this morning, aren't you?"

"Uh-huh," Keisha replied. "But I wanted to let you know that I might be late." She told Alison about her plan to check Ellie's book collection for ideas.

"Good thinking!" Alison exclaimed. "Why don't you talk to Ellie, too? She'll probably have dozens of suggestions for you."

Keisha sighed. "That's what I thought," she said. "Except it turns out that Ellie has out-of-town guests this weekend, and she's going to be busy with them all day. But she said I could come over and look through her books. She's leaving me a key under the mat."

"It's too bad that Ellie won't be there, but I bet you'll still find something to help you," Alison said reassuringly. "Ellie's house is always full of surprises, whether she's there or not."

Chapter
Three

BOOKS, BOOKS, AND MORE BOOKS

eisha gazed around Ellie's sitting room. "Wow," she murmured to herself, her eyes roaming over shelf after shelf. "I never noticed there were so many books in here."

The sitting room was a favorite spot of all the girls. Its walls were covered in burgundy and gold striped wallpaper and dark paneling, and gold-framed paintings adorned the wall above the deep, brick-lined fireplace. Shelves were crammed into every possible space, and the

books on them were often packed
two layers deep.

Keisha peered at some of the
titles. There were books about
music, books about the theater,
books about travel, works of fiction
and poetry, and, last but not least,
lots and lots of books about history.

Keisha wandered around
the room. She had no idea
where to start looking for topic
ideas. Ellie seemed to have almost as many books as the
public library!

"Maybe I should just go to the library," Keisha
muttered under her breath. "At least there I'd have some
help looking." Still she couldn't shake the feeling that the
perfect idea was right there in that room, waiting for her.

Keisha looked at the books one more time, then
wandered out into the entry hall, not sure what to do. She
glanced around uncertainly. The house was strangely quiet
and empty. Ellie had gone out with her guests, taking her
dog, Monty, along. Usually, even when Ellie wasn't home,
Keisha loved playing with the friendly white terrier.

Then her gaze fell on the small table opposite the
front door. A silver box rested on its smooth, polished
surface. Keisha didn't have to open the box to know what

was inside. It was the key to the attic. Ellie left it there so the girls could use it any time they wanted to.

Tempted, Keisha looked at her watch. It was still early. She wasn't supposed to meet her friends at the library for almost an hour. And anyway, she'd told Alison that she might be a little late.

That made up her mind. She hurried to the table. Seconds later she was carefully unlocking the door to the attic. The bright morning sun pouring through the dormer windows illuminated every corner of the wide, comfortable room, so Keisha didn't bother reaching for the satin cord of the hanging lamp. Instead she headed straight for the old steamer trunk at one end of the room. She barely glanced at the piles of old luggage, the cluttered mahogany desk, or any of the other souvenirs of Ellie's life and travels.

Keisha heaved open the trunk's lid, then knelt on the soft oriental rug to look inside. One of the most interesting things about the trunk was that the girls never seemed to find the same outfits twice in its roomy depths.

Keisha pulled out one piece of clothing after another: a pair of green tights, a sparkly pink ball gown, long black velvet gloves.

Then a flash of her favorite color caught her eye. She shoved aside the clothes on top and reached for the purple fabric. As soon as she held it up, she gasped. It was

a lavender dress, short and sassy, made of soft, sparkly fabric with layers of fringe at the bottom. For a second, she couldn't figure out why the dress seemed so familiar. Had she or one of her friends worn it on a past adventure? Had she seen it in the trunk on a previous visit?

Then she remembered. The dress looked almost exactly like the ones her great-grandmother and her friend wore in that old picture in the family photo album.

"It's beautiful!" Keisha said softly, turning the dress this way and that. Glancing into the trunk again, she saw a pair of lavender shoes poking out in the spot where the dress had been. Next to the shoes, was a long, lavender-colored pearl necklace and a beaded purse of the same color. Tucked into the top of the purse was a pair of white cotton gloves. A lavender headband decorated with a matching feather lay nearby atop a pair of pale purple stockings.

Keisha set the small pile of clothes on a chair near the trunk and stared at it. "I shouldn't," she told herself out loud. She stared at the outfit for another moment. She had so much work to do if she wanted to get a good grade on her project, she really didn't have time for fun, like trying on this outfit and seeing what happened. She should get started at the library right away, even though her friends wouldn't be there for half an hour.

Still, Keisha hesitated. She ran her fingers over the

shiny fabric of the dress. And the fringe, it was so pretty. Surely it couldn't hurt…

Before she knew it, she had changed out of her regular clothes and into the fancy dress. It fit perfectly, hanging straight down from her shoulders, and swinging about her legs an inch or two above her knees. The stockings and the chunky-heeled shoes fit, too. Keisha slipped the necklace over her head before putting on the headpiece and gloves and picking up the beaded handbag.

She smiled. Just wearing the jaunty little dress made her feel happier somehow. She couldn't help skipping as she went over to the full-length mirror to see how she looked.

"Wow," she murmured, running her eyes over her reflection. "I look like I'm ready to go dancing or something."

Suddenly, the image of the room behind her shimmered and changed. The bright morning light faded as quickly as if the sun had darted behind a cloud bank, and the details of the room were lost in shadow.

Keisha's eyes adjusted quickly to the dim light. Looking around, she saw that she was standing in a tiny room. A bed was pushed against one wall. Opposite was a rickety-looking bureau, next to a partially closed door. A tub full of plants stood in front of the only window in the room.

Keisha was about to go over to the window and look

out when she heard sounds from the next room. Was that someone calling her name?

chapter Four

WELCOME TO HARLEM

eisha!" It was a woman's voice, strong and rich. "Keisha, honey, where'd you get to?"

"I'm right here." Keisha crossed the room in three steps, pushed the door open, and found herself face to face with a stylish, strangely familiar woman in a colorful old-fashioned silky dress. Keisha almost gasped. It was the woman from the fuzzy old photograph in her family's album—her great-grandmother's friend who lived in New York City in the 1920s! What was her name again?

The woman's face broke into a delighted smile. "Oh, Keisha, honey!" she exclaimed. "That dress is the berries! It looks like it was made for you, or my name's not Norma Frances Callister."

Yes, that's the name, Keisha thought. That's the woman my parents were talking about! Keisha glanced down at her outfit and smiled. "Thanks," she said. "It fits perfectly." She wriggled her hips back and forth slightly to set the hem of the dress dancing. Meanwhile, she glanced around the room. It was much larger and brighter than the bedroom. Several tall bookcases towered over a messy desk, and an ancient but comfortable-looking low sofa stretched across the space in front of the wide windows. Stacks of books covered the coffee table and one of the end tables that flanked the sofa. A second end table held a large, old-fashioned gramophone and piles of recordings. The walls of the room were covered with so many paintings and photographs and framed letters that Keisha could hardly see the sky-blue wallpaper behind them.

"I had a feeling it would fit you," Norma went on. "I was at a party recently and spotted a young lady wearing one just like it. Miss Zora Hurston, a fine acquaintance of mine, convinced me I should get myself one, so I did. Never mind that it ended up being three sizes too small!" She let out another peal of amused laughter.

Keisha wrinkled her forehead as she tried to figure out why the name Norma had mentioned sounded so familiar. Then she gasped as she remembered: Norma was talking about Zora Neale Hurston, a famous author! Keisha's parents had one of her novels in their "favorite books" pile beside their bed. "Do you really know Zora Neale Hurston?" she asked breathlessly.

"Honey, I know everyone." Norma laughed her strong, infectious laugh again. She waved a hand to indicate the room they were in. "This place may not look like much, but the fine minds and musical talents of Harlem surely do love to hang about here and talk about everything and nothing. Langston Hughes, Fats Waller, Countee Cullen, the lot of them. They've all wandered through at one point or another." She shook her head. "And I swear, some of them think they own the old place."

Keisha glanced around the room again. She couldn't blame anybody, even famous people, for liking it. It had a cozy, welcoming feeling that probably had something to do with the slightly worn, comfortable furnishings and a lot to do with its friendly, down-to-earth hostess. Even though she was talking about the famous writers and musicians she knew, Norma didn't sound snobbish at all. She talked about famous people the way Keisha might talk about her school friends.

Norma smiled and waved a hand. "Before we get to gabbing anymore, why don't you go change out of that dress?" she suggested. "You don't want to wrinkle it, or it won't be ready when you're ready to wear it someplace special."

"Um, okay," Keisha said uncertainly. She backed through the doorway behind her and looked around the tiny bedroom. For the first time, she noticed that there was a dress lying on the bed, much plainer than the one she was wearing, as well as matching shoes and a jacket. She quickly slipped out of the lavender dress, hanging it carefully over a chair, and slipped on the other clothes. Even though they were much more ordinary, they felt almost as exotic and special. Keisha glanced at herself in the wavy mirror over the old bureau and smiled. She could hardly wait to see what happened next.

She hurried back to the main room. "Is this better?" she asked Norma, twirling around for her inspection.

Norma looked up and smiled. "Solid, honey," she said. She was seated at a desk so overloaded with papers, books, and trinkets that it seemed about to collapse. She picked up an envelope and waved it. "This is the article I need you to take over to the magazine office," she told

Keisha. "Are you sure you don't mind running it down the street for me? I know this is supposed to be your school vacation. Your mama'll be as mad as a hornet if I turn you into my assistant while you're visiting."

"It's okay," Keisha said. "I don't mind at all. What's the article about?"

"It's a review of the latest performance by Mr. Louis Armstrong," Norma said. "I know you're not from these parts, so maybe you haven't heard of him yet. But you will, mark my words. His music could set a dead man dancing."

Keisha smiled. She liked the way Norma talked. Also,

she did know who Louis Armstrong was. He was a very famous trumpet player. Her parents listened to his music all the time. "Where's the office?" she asked.

Norma grabbed a scrap of paper off her desk and started scribbling on it. "I'll write down some directions for you, honey. But if you get yourself lost, just ask anyone for the offices of *Harlem Rhythm*. It's the most bodacious new magazine uptown. Very hot." She looked up and winked as she handed Keisha the scrawled directions and a large envelope. "And I should know. I've written for just about all of them. *Opportunity*, *New York Age*, even *The Crisis*. I'll tell you, Keisha, these magazines are changing the way the world looks at us up here in Harlem. Whoever would've thought that someone like little old me would be a part of it all?" She threw her arms wide and let out a loud, delighted peal of laughter.

Keisha grinned at Norma's enthusiasm. Then she glanced at the sheet of paper. "Sounds pretty important," she said, tucking the envelope under one arm. "I'll take it right over."

Norma chuckled. "Don't worry, honey, there's no rush," she said. "Feel free to explore a little. You just got here, and I'm sure you'll be wanting to see what Harlem's all about. On your way down to the office you may want to look around Seventh Avenue—you could say it's the heart of Harlem. We're on St. Nicholas Avenue here, so head a couple of blocks east and you're there. Hey, I have an idea—when you get to the magazine's office, ask for my good friend, John. He knows so much about the neighborhood and he loves to show it off! Tell him I said to give you a little tour."

Keisha left the apartment and made her way down a dimly lit black-and-white-tiled hallway and down two flights of stairs. Crossing a small lobby, she pushed open one of the heavy double doors.

She stepped outside, and found Harlem all around her. It was so big and bustling and alive, it almost took her breath away. She started walking slowly up St. Nicholas Avenue to the end of the block, where she turned right to head east. Most of the buildings she passed were set close together, narrow and high. Many of them had intricately scrolled cornices and pediments above their doors and windows, and some had interesting carvings or even gargoyles across their crowns. Awnings and flags waved lazily in the light breeze winding its way down the sidewalk, gaudily colored curtains fluttered through open windows, and the sounds of talk, laughter, and music poured out of almost every building.

But that was nothing compared to what was going on in the street around her. Once she found Seventh Avenue, Keisha turned left to head north, as Norma's directions specified. Keisha didn't think she'd ever seen so many people in one place. Old and young, fat and thin, rich and poor—they all seemed to be there. The only things they had in common were that almost every one of them was African-American, just like her, and that they all seemed to be thoroughly enjoying the warm, sunny afternoon. The women were wearing all sorts of colorful and interesting outfits. There were lots of floaty dresses, bright patterned shawls, and dainty parasols. Some of the women and girls wore simple but pretty gingham frocks. Others had fancy hats with huge white feathers waving out of the brims. A few even sashayed past in dresses similar to the lavender one Keisha had been wearing. Lots of the men and boys were in clothing as fancy as the women. They wore striped pants with white spats, or checkered suits. Some twirled fancy walking sticks as they strolled down the avenue.

There was so much to look at, listen to, and even smell—especially from the crowded, noisy restaurants along the avenue—that for a while Keisha forgot what she was supposed to be doing. She just wandered up Seventh Avenue, trying to take it all in and commit every detail to memory.

But finally she remembered her errand. She still had Norma's envelope tucked under her arm. Pulling the directions from her pocket, she reluctantly turned her attention away from the lively street scene and started peering up at the addresses on the buildings that surrounded her.

"Looking for something, miss?" a polite voice came from behind her.

Keisha turned and saw an African-American girl of about seventeen standing on a corner. She had short black hair and was dressed in a bright red dress and matching hat. A stack of papers was balanced in the crook of her arm.

Keisha smiled tentatively. "I'm looking for the office of *Harlem Rhythm* magazine. I think it should be around here somewhere."

The young woman's face lit up. "It sure is," she said. She pointed to a narrow brick building across the street. "It's right over there. Second floor." She grabbed one of the papers from the stack she was holding and handed it to Keisha. "And here's one more piece of advice. If you want to have fun and hear some really solid music, come to the contest tonight."

"Contest?" Keisha asked curiously. "What contest?" She glanced at the flyer in her hand.

"It's a contest for young

musicians," the girl explained eagerly. "It's only a few blocks from here." She winked at Keisha. "There'll be fun and dancing for everyone, young and old. And there's a special secret prize for the winning band."

"A secret prize?" Keisha felt a flutter of excitement in her stomach. That sounded interesting—like something Norma might write about for one of the Harlem magazines she had talked about. "Thanks," she said. "For the directions *and* the advice!"

Chapter

Five

PROMENADES
AND PRIZES

 few minutes later Keisha cautiously stuck her head around the corner of an open door. Inside the second-floor apartment that matched the address on Norma's envelope, she found a makeshift office. Several desks were lined up near the windows on the far side of the main room, and several men and women were reading or writing or typing busily. Lively music from a phonograph in the middle of the room filled the air. A young man of about twenty was lounging in an armchair near the door. He tapped his foot to the soft music as he sorted through a large stack of mail.

"Um—is this the office of *Harlem Rhythm* magazine?" Keisha asked uncertainly.

The fellow looked up. "You got it, sister. This is the place."

"Oh, good." Keisha stepped inside and took a closer look around. The adults across the room gave her a quick glance, then returned to their work. Keisha noticed that the walls were covered with newspaper clippings, black and white photos, brightly colored posters, and all sorts of other papers. Stacks of books and magazines filled much of the extra floor space. "Um, Norma Callister sent me," Keisha said. "Here. This is from her." She handed the envelope to the man.

He took it and gave Keisha a quizzical look. "You work for Norma?" he asked, sounding impressed. "Solid. She's a fine lady. Knows everyone and everything there is to know in Harlem. You must be new around here."

"I'm just visiting from out of town," Keisha explained. "My name's Keisha and Norma told me to speak to her friend, John."

He stuck out his hand. "You're speaking to him! It's a pleasure to make your acquaintance, Keisha. I'm John. Is this your first time in Harlem?"

Keisha nodded. "I just got here. It's amazing. This place is jumping!" she added, repeating an expression she'd heard from Norma.

John laughed. "You got that right, Keisha," he agreed. "Hey, I'm due for a break here. I'm just helping out my cousin—he's the editor of this magazine." He jerked a thumb over his shoulder to indicate a young man at one of the desks. "What do you say I show you around?"

"That sounds great!" Keisha said quickly. "Thanks! Norma said you were a good tour guide." She was eager to see more of Harlem.

John went over to speak to his cousin, then rejoined Keisha at the entrance. "Ready," he announced. "Let's go."

Keisha and John strolled around the neighborhood, talking and laughing. Keisha asked lots of questions about life in Harlem. John had lived there all his life, so he knew most of the answers. He told her that people loved parading up and down Seventh Avenue, especially on Sundays after church. He called it "promenading." Keisha also asked John questions about himself, and soon found out that he was a musician.

"I play trumpet in a little combo made up of some

guys from my block," he explained, smiling a little shyly. "We call ourselves Johnny's Showstoppers. Someday I'd love to get a gig playing one of the big Harlem clubs. It's my dream." He sighed. "Just picture it. Me on stage, playing with someone like Fats Waller, Bessie Smith, maybe even Louis Armstrong—he's my idol."

"Who knows? It might happen soon," Keisha said. "Has your band played anywhere yet?"

John shrugged. "Actually, we're entered in a contest up on 138th Street tonight. It's our first public performance."

Keisha remembered the young woman on the street. "Is that the musicians' contest?" she asked. "I just heard about it. I was going to see if Norma wanted to write an article about it for your cousin's magazine."

"Really? Solid! It should be enormously hot," John said eagerly. "Especially if what they say about the prize is true."

"Prize?" Keisha repeated. "You mean the big secret prize?"

John nodded and grinned. "I heard a rumor that the winning band goes home with a fistful of diamonds."

"Wow!" Keisha gasped. "That's some prize!"

"You're telling me," John

declared, dodging his way around a laughing trio of boys playing around a streetlamp. "The contest is being sponsored by a rich old lady named Miss Bunting who lives up on Striver's Row, so I guess she can probably afford as many diamonds as she wants to give away. But I'm not counting on anything. I heard another rumor that the prize is just a little gold cup or a bunch of flowers or something." He grinned wider than ever. "I even heard it might be a racehorse! Can you picture it? A thorough-bred—here in Harlem."

Keisha laughed at the thought. The more she heard about this contest, the more interesting it sounded. She was sure Norma would be interested, too. She tried to remember what kinds of questions reporters asked in situations like this. "Where did you hear about the prizes?" she asked John.

"My older brother told me everyone was syndicating about the contest at the rent party he went to last night," John explained.

"Syndicating? Rent party?" Keisha repeated, feeling confused. People in Harlem had such a funny way of talking sometimes—almost like a totally different language. It could be hard to follow their meaning.

The boy gave her a surprised look, then laughed. "Oh, I forgot," he said. "You're from out of town, right? You don't know the lingo. Syndicating means, you know, woofing. Gossiping. You dig?"

Keisha nodded.

"And I guess they probably don't have rent parties wherever you come from," John went on. "That's what it's called when someone throws a party and charges admission to get some money together before the rent comes due."

"Oh." Keisha smiled. "I guess that makes sense." She made a mental note of everything John had told her about the contest. Then she went back to looking around and enjoying herself. "Where are we heading, anyway?" she asked.

"Nowhere special," John replied. "Just strolling." Suddenly his face lit up, and he broke into his wide grin again. "Hey, I've got an idea," he said. "Why don't we head over to the Tree of Life? I could use a little luck tonight."

Once again, Keisha had no idea what he was talking about. "Where?" she asked.

"Oh, right. Out-of-towner." John crooked a finger at her, gesturing for her to follow him. He hurried down the street. "Come on. I'll show you. It's on 131st Street."

A few minutes later, they stopped in front of a large tree. "Is this it?" Keisha asked.

John nodded. As Keisha watched, he reached out and rubbed the bark on the tree trunk. "This is what we call the Tree of Life," he explained. "If you're a musician

looking for a break, they say it helps to give it a rub." He smiled and winked. "I don't know if I believe it," he told Keisha in a low voice. "But what I say is, it sure can't hurt!"

Keisha laughed. She reached out and touched the rough bark. "You never know what can happen," she said.

They left the tree and continued walking. Keisha craned her neck, trying to see absolutely everything. She gazed up at the tops of the buildings. She watched the constantly changing parade of people pouring past. She peered into storefronts. Suddenly she spotted a clock inside a restaurant and gasped. "Uh-oh," she said. "It's getting late. I want to get back to Norma's and tell her about the contest."

John nodded. "I dig," he said. "Come on, I'll show you a shortcut."

A few minutes later, a breathless Keisha burst into Norma's apartment. "I'm back!" she called.

Norma appeared from a doorway at the back of the main room. "Oh, Keisha, honey," she cried. "I'm glad you're back. I forgot to tell you I'm supposed to visit a sick friend tonight. I hope you don't mind doing your own thing for dinner." She looked worried. "Maybe I can get one of the neighbors to feed you."

"That's okay," Keisha answered quickly. She was disappointed to hear that Norma was busy that evening.

That meant she couldn't go to the music contest. But suddenly she had a wonderful idea. She told Norma about the contest, showing her the flyer the girl had given her.

"Hmm," Norma said as Keisha finished. She shrugged and laughed. "It could just be an excuse for another party. That's Harlem for you. But it does sound interesting. Miss Bunting gets some crazy ideas in that rich old head of hers sometimes. If anyone would decide to present a pony as a prize for a music contest, it would just about have to be her."

"I was going to see if you wanted to go and write an article about it," Keisha went on. She crossed her fingers behind her back. "But since you're busy tonight, maybe I can go—and write the article myself."

Norma looked surprised. Then she looked thoughtful. "Well, now," she murmured. "That's quite an idea." She studied the flyer carefully.

Keisha held her breath. Would Norma let her go?

Finally Norma smiled. "All right," she said decisively. "You're a big girl. I think you can handle it. And I can walk you there on my way to my friend's place."

Keisha let out a whoop and punched her fist in the air. Then she rushed forward to hug Norma. "Thanks!" she cried. "I'll write the best article you ever saw. I promise."

"That's good, honey." Norma laughed and hugged her back. "We'd better hurry now. We'll have to be leaving

soon. Why don't you go and put on that purple dress?"
she added. "I have a matching shawl in case it's chilly,
and a hat to keep your hair neat. The contest is the
perfect occasion for a pretty outfit like that."

"Thanks, Norma." Keisha turned toward the small
bedroom where her beautiful dress was waiting. She
couldn't stop thinking about how exciting it would be to
see John's band and all the other talented young
musicians—and maybe find out the real story behind
that mysterious prize.

Chapter
Six

IT'S SHOWTIME!

Keisha straightened her shoulders and stood as tall as she could. She waved as Norma hurried away. She had arrived! This was the building where the contest was taking place. She gazed up at the scrolled decorations above the arched stone doorway for a moment. Then she pushed open the broad wooden doors and entered the music hall. A few seconds later she found herself in a cavernous room. The stage spanned the far end, and large round tables were scattered in the area near the entrance. In between lay the wide, smooth, polished expanse of the wooden dance floor. Lights twinkled from the ceiling far above her, as well as from the candles that seemed to be everywhere.

Everyone in Harlem seemed to have turned out for the contest, from kids and teenagers to elderly ladies and gentlemen leaning on canes. People were talking and laughing and shouting to their friends and neighbors. A group of young girls was dancing around at the edge of the dance floor, even though there wasn't any music playing yet. Keisha smiled as she watched them swish their dresses back and forth and giggle. They were having fun already—and so was she!

She pushed her way to a spot where she could see the stage. Several young men were dragging instruments into place. Another man was setting up a microphone near the front of the stage.

"Hi, there," said a familiar voice behind her. "You made it."

Keisha turned and saw the girl who had first told her about the contest. Two teenage boys were standing with her. "Hi," Keisha said breathlessly. "This is so exciting. I'm so glad I came."

The girl grinned and gestured at the boys. "Me, too. I even dragged my brothers along." Someone let out a shout nearby, and the girl glanced over. "Oh, there's my boyfriend. I'd better go. Have fun!" With a wave, she and her brothers disappeared into the crowd.

Keisha didn't mind. There was so much to look at. She was amazed by all the fancy, very dressy clothes. Some of the musicians were even wearing tuxedos—including one little boy who couldn't have been more than five years old! He was holding a big trombone. Keisha watched him until she was distracted by a beautiful, exotic-looking girl about her own age in a sparkling ballgown that seemed to be made of a million diamonds. There was so much to watch that Keisha hardly noticed that time was passing. She was startled when the man on stage introduced the first band.

As the lively music started and a teenage girl stepped to the microphone and began singing, Keisha remembered that she had a job to do. She was supposed to be finding out about the evening's prize. She was, after all, a reporter—at least for one night.

She pulled out the notebook and pen Norma had lent her. Many of the spectators were on the dance floor, so there was a little more space among the tables. Keisha wandered around, wondering how to start. She tried asking a few people what they knew about the prizes. Some people didn't know anything. Others had heard the same rumors as John.

"Keisha!" called a friendly voice over the music. "You made it!"

Keisha turned and saw John waving at her from a table a short distance away. He was sitting with several other young men, all dressed in dark blue suits, most of them with large black cases at their feet; one had the words *Johnny's Showstoppers* painted on its side.

Keisha waved back. "Good luck!" she called.

As she turned away from John's table, she caught sight of an older woman sitting at another table directly in her line of sight. Keisha's jaw dropped. The woman had to be one of the most unusual people she had ever seen. Her hair was snow white. She wore a bright red turban with a dramatic brooch pinned on one side. She was dressed in a shimmery gold gown. Her hands were bejeweled. Bracelets and necklaces were draped by the dozens around her thin arms and neck. She surveyed the crowd with quiet dignity and sharp dark eyes.

The woman noticed Keisha staring. She raised one of her fingers and gestured for her to approach. Keisha gulped and obeyed. She hoped her staring hadn't seemed too rude. But she had never seen anyone as fancily and expensively dressed as this old woman.

"Hello, child," the woman said in a raspy voice as

Keisha drew closer. "I don't remember seeing you around these parts."

Keisha quickly introduced herself. "I'm staying with Norma—I mean, Miss Callister," she explained. "I'm writing an article about the contest for *Harlem Rhythm* magazine."

"I see." The old woman nodded. "Well, it's a pleasure to make your acquaintance, young Keisha. My name is Belle Bunting."

Keisha's eyes widened. Miss Bunting! This woman was the wealthy sponsor of the contest. "It's great to meet you," she said politely. "Um—would you mind if I ask you a question?"

"Not at all." Miss Bunting smiled. "Ask away, child."

Keisha took a deep breath and summoned all her confidence. "I heard there's a special prize for the winner tonight," she said in a rush. "Can you please tell me what it is?"

Miss Bunting leaned forward slightly and her smile widened. "What have you heard?"

Keisha told her. She was surprised when the old woman burst into peals of fragile but genuine laughter.

"Oh, my!" Miss Bunting raised one thin, shaky hand to wipe away a teardrop. "I might have known something like this would happen. People in Harlem can't resist wagging their tongues when there's gossip to be spread!"

"Does that mean the rumors are wrong?" Keisha felt

slightly disappointed. "There's no big prize?"

Miss Bunting looked around to make sure no one was close enough to overhear. "Not at all, my dear," she assured Keisha. "Can you keep a secret?"

"Sure," Keisha said quickly. She glanced down at her notebook. "Um, I mean, I was hoping I could put it in my article—"

Miss Bunting cut her off with a wave of her hand. "Don't worry your head about that," she assured Keisha. "You and my friend Norma Callister and everybody else in Harlem can write whatever you please about my contest once the prize has been awarded." She winked at Keisha. "No, you just have to keep my secret until the end of tonight."

"Oh." Keisha grinned. "That's easy. I promise."

"Good." Miss Bunting indicated the chair beside her, and Keisha sat down. "Now," the old lady said, "first I'll explain where your rumors came from. You see, I told one close friend I was setting up a special prize for the young performers tonight." She nodded toward the stage, where a tall, slender young man was tap-dancing while three musicians played enthusiastically behind him. "But I wouldn't tell my friend exactly what I had in mind, because I wasn't certain I could actually make it happen. So I just told him it would be something worth more than diamonds or gold to a real musician. I seem to recall I also said it would be better to a young performer than a field full of flowers or horses." She chuckled. "I guess I was trying to be poetic. Even an old lady like me gets carried away sometimes."

"Oh!" Now Keisha understood. It reminded her of a party game where everyone lined up in a row. The first person whispered something to the next in line, that person whispered to the next, and so on. By the time the message reached the end of the line, it was usually completely different. She giggled. "So that's where all those rumors about ponies and diamonds came from."

Miss Bunting nodded, smiling. "That's right. And now you, young Keisha, will be the first in this place to find out the real prize." She bent closer and whispered in Keisha's ear.

Keisha's eyes widened as she heard the truth about the prize. "That's amazing!" she exclaimed. "No wonder you wanted to surprise everyone."

Miss Bunting smiled again and winked. "Don't tell a soul," she whispered.

Keisha talked with Miss Bunting for a few more minutes. When she heard the master of ceremonies announce John's band, she said good-bye to Miss Bunting and went to find a good place to watch.

C h a p t e r

Seven

THE PERFECT TOPIC

eople were standing near the tables watching the dancers, and many of them were taller than Keisha. She had trouble finding a spot where she could see. First she tried hopping up and down to get a view. Then she tried peering between people. But it was no use.

Then John's band began. Their first song was zippy and fast, and it made Keisha's foot start tapping almost without her realizing it. That gave her an idea: Why not watch from the dance floor?

She pushed her way through the crowd. People were dancing alone or in pairs, arms and legs flashing, women's dresses flying. Keisha grinned and plunged right in. She loved to dance, and it was even more fun with the music of Johnny's Showstoppers pouring off the stage, the swingy skirt of Norma's lavender dress flying around her legs, and the energy-filled air of the dance hall all around.

"Hi!" someone shouted.

Keisha turned to see the girl from the street once again. Her boyfriend and her brothers were dancing beside her. "Hi!" Keisha called back, struggling to make herself heard over the blaring trumpets and saxophones onstage. "This is fun!"

"Come do the Charleston with us!" the girl cried, pulling Keisha into the circle with her. She showed her how to swing her arms and move her feet in time with the bouncy rhythm.

After that, Keisha danced the popular dance without stopping, catching her breath in between acts. It was the most fun she had had in a long time. The rest of the evening flew by. Keisha could hardly believe it when the emcee announced that it was time to present the award to the best performer of the evening.

Everyone crowded onto the dance floor to watch as a judge handed the announcer a white envelope. Keisha could see John standing with his band across the crowded

room, and she crossed her fingers for him. She thought his band had been the best of all the wonderful performers.

The emcee slit open the envelope and read the card inside. "Ladies and gentlemen!" he cried with a flourish. "I'm thrilled to announce that the winner of tonight's grand prize is—" he paused, and the entire crowded hall was silent, waiting for his next words; finally he went on—"Johnny's Showstoppers!"

Keisha gasped. Then she starting clapping wildly. John's band had won!

John and his friends were grinning ear to ear as they climbed on stage to take their bows. Keisha was grinning, too—especially since she knew what was coming next.

"But wait, there's more!" the emcee exclaimed as the boys waved at the crowd. "I haven't told you what you've won." He paused dramatically for a moment before continuing. "But perhaps I should let the prize speak for itself."

Keisha held her breath along with everyone else. Even though she already knew what the announcer was going to say, it was an exciting moment.

The emcee smiled. "And that's because the prize is

one night playing at the world-famous Connie's Inn
with Mr. Louis Armstrong himself! Here he is
now to tell you all about it!" The emcee
swept his arm toward the side of the
stage, and a well dressed young
man with smooth, dark skin
strode on, waving his trumpet at
the excited crowd.

Keisha watched John. He looked
just as excited as she had known he would, and she was
thrilled that his dream would be coming true even sooner
than he had hoped. She looked over at Louis Armstrong
and smiled as she wondered what her parents would
think if they could see her now, standing only a few yards
away from one of the most famous musicians of the
twentieth century. Suddenly she realized that if she
wanted to be a real reporter, she should try to interview
him for her article. She pushed her way to the edge of the
stage and managed to get John's attention.

He hurried over to her, his dark eyes bright with
excitement. "Can you believe this?" he exclaimed. "This
is the best prize in the world! I can't believe we won!"

"I can," Keisha said with a grin. "You were great. But
listen, do you think Mr. Armstrong would talk to me for
my article?"

John reached down to help her onstage. "Let's go ask him."

Keisha's eyes strayed to the clock on Norma's wall. It was getting late, and she was beginning to realize that she should be getting back to Ellie's. She had been working hard on her article ever since returning from the dance hall, and it was just about finished. But she knew she had another writing assignment to do back home, and she was looking forward to getting started on it.

Keisha finished the last few sentences, ending with a quote from Louis Armstrong about the contest. It had been exciting to interview him, especially since he had been as nice as could be. When she had written the last word, she set down her pen, gathered the article into a neat stack of papers, and left it right in the center of Norma's desk.

"I hope you like it, Norma," she whispered, taking one last glance at the first page. She turned to look around the cozy, cluttered room, then wandered over toward the window overlooking St. Nicholas Avenue. Outside, the streetlights were casting a golden-yellow glow over all of Harlem, and Keisha knew that Norma would be home soon. She gazed out at the city, listening to the faint sounds of laughter and music that still drifted by on the lazy evening breeze.

Finally she turned away. She would miss Harlem—its life, its spirit, its music, and most of all its people. But she knew she would always remember them. She smoothed the skirt of her lavender dress and went into the small bathroom, where she stared into the mirror over the sink and waited.

Chapter
Eight

HOME AGAIN

moment later Keisha blinked and looked around.
She was back in Ellie's attic, which seemed very still
and quiet and sleepy after the excitement of Harlem.

She took one last look at herself in the mirror, then
reluctantly changed out of the beautiful lavender outfit
and tucked it carefully back in place in the deep old trunk.
She sat back on her heels for a moment, still thinking
about her adventure. It had taught her a lot, and it had
given her a perfect idea for her school assignment. But

just as important, it had been a lot of fun. She knew she would never forget a second of this adventure, or of the hard-working, hard-playing people she had met.

Keisha hoped that Norma liked her article. And she especially hoped that John had the time of his life when he played with Louis Armstrong. But she could think more about those things later. Right now she had something else to do.

She skipped downstairs, still humming a scrap of the music John's band had played in the contest. She returned the attic key to its box, then hurried back into Ellie's sitting room. This time there was no confusion or hesitation in her step as she moved around the room. Now she had a much better idea about what she was looking for. She scanned the bookshelves, picked out several books that looked interesting and tucked them into her bookbag.

On her way out, Keisha glanced at the clock over the fireplace. She was later than she expected, and by now her friends might be worried about her. She quickly pulled Ellie's door closed and locked it. Then she returned the house key to its hiding spot.

"Keisha!"

"Hey, Keish!"

Keisha looked up, surprised to hear voices calling her name. Her four best friends were hurrying up the driveway toward her.

"You were late so we came after you," Rose called.

Alison nodded. "We thought you might need some help sorting through the books at Ellie's house."

Keisha smiled. What great friends I have, she thought. "Thanks, you guys, but guess what? I've already figured out what I'm going to write about." Keisha filled them in on her exciting adventure in Harlem. "You would have loved being there, too," she went on. "The Harlem Renaissance was such an interesting time in history for African-Americans. Lots of famous writers and poets hung out in Harlem—and the music..." She shook her head, remembering the contest for young musicians and the way the hall had rocked. "You should have heard John play the trumpet. We were all dancing and moving..."

Before she realized what she was doing, she'd put down her bookbag, grabbed Heather and Megan by the hand and began to swing their arms in time with hers. "Come on, you guys," she said, moving her feet forward and then backward.

"I'll teach you how to do the Charleston."

"Cool!" Alison said eagerly. "I've seen my aunt and uncle do that dance. It always looks like so much fun."

"It is," Keisha agreed, demonstrating.

Her friends picked up the dance in no time. Keisha glanced back toward Ellie's house, wishing that their friend was home. Ellie would certainly enjoy the sight of the five of them doing the Charleston in her driveway. Knowing Ellie, Keisha thought with a smile, she'd probably come out and join us!

Diary

Dear Diary,

Guess what? I got an A+ on my history assignment!

I'm really happy about that. I worked hard on my paper. I think it's because I loved learning all about the people who lived during the Harlem Renaissance—famous writers like Zora Neale Hurston, Langston Hughes, and Countee Cullen, really smart thinkers like W. E. B. DuBois, and musicians like Bessie Smith, Fats Waller, and of course Louis Armstrong. Those famous artists and thinkers did a lot to convince the world that African-Americans could be just as creative and talented as anyone else. I guess history isn't just about wars and terrible stuff after all.

My dad was really glad I found such a

great topic for my paper. He's sure that I got the idea from his showing me that picture of Norma in the photo album. (Well, it's sort of true, isn't it?) The other day, he and I spent a lot of time listening to music from Louis Armstrong and the other musicians who were around then, and I really liked all of it. Some of it even reminded me of Johnny's Showstoppers. Pretty cool—or, should I say, bodacious!

Anyway, Ms. Austin said she thought my paper was one of the best I ever wrote. She even asked me to read it to the class. Everyone was really interested, especially since most of them had never even heard of the Harlem Renaissance. It was exciting to teach people about something new. Maybe if I decide not to become a doctor or a nurse or a paramedic, I'll be a teacher. Anything's possible, right?

Later, Diary!

Keisha